...tale News

ONCE UPON A TIME AND EVER AFTER!

...D!

...WOLF

...GHTGOWN

...IN BIG TROUBLE AGAIN!

...claims that it is quite usual for him to ...ear these things while he is relaxing.

"There ain't no law that says a wolf can't wear a nightgown," he growled. "I like pretty things. It's always the same; wolves get blamed for everything. I haven't done anything wrong!"

B.B. Wolf added that he is consulting his lawyers, Tweedledum & Tweedledee, about the unprovoked attack on his person by Mr. Hood.

What a HOWLER! BB Wolf feels the long arm of the law

KISS ME QUICK!

...OCKS

Fairytale News

For the arrival of Summer

First U.S. edition 2004

Library of Congress Cataloging-in-Publication Data is available.

Library of Congress Catalog Card Number 2003048503

ISBN 0-7636-2166-8

10 9 8 7 6 5 4 3 2 3 1

Printed in China

This book was typeset in Aunt Mildred.
The illustrations were done in watercolor.

Candlewick Press
2067 Massachusetts Avenue
Cambridge, Massachusetts 02140

visit us at www.candlewick.com

Fairytale News

Colin & Jacqui Hawkins

CANDLEWICK PRESS
CAMBRIDGE, MASSACHUSETTS

Once upon a time, in an old tumbledown cottage on the edge of Tangled Wood, lived Mother Hubbard with her son, Jack.

One morning Mother Hubbard went to the cupboard, but the cupboard was bare.
"What shall we do?" she cried. "We've no food and no money. Jack, you'll have to find a job or we'll starve."

So Jack scooted off into town. He looked all over for work.

He tried
PORKERS THE BUTCHERS.

Then he tried
WAX & WAYNE.

And then he tried the
PAT-A-CAKE BAKERY.
Poor Jack couldn't
get a job anywhere.

Just then he saw a sign in the Tittle Tattle News Shop window, saying PAPERBOY/GIRL WANTED. APPLY WITHIN. So in Jack rushed.

Mrs. Tattle was delighted. "The job's yours," she said, and gave Jack a big bag of the FAIRYTALE NEWS to deliver.

Jack scurried off happily. "I'm going to be the best paperboy ever!" he said.

Jack's first delivery was to the home of the Three Bears, who lived at Honey Cottage on Hickory Lane.

PORKERS

Inside Honey Cottage, the Three Bears were about to have breakfast when Jack slid the newspaper through the mail slot.

Mr. Bear picked up the paper and sat down at the kitchen table.

"What's for breakfast, Mom?" asked Baby Bear.

"It's your favorite," said Mrs. Bear.

"Porridge!" shouted Baby Bear.

Mr. Bear put down his paper and they all began to eat their porridge, but it was much too hot.
"Never mind," said Mrs. Bear.
"Let's all go for a walk while it cools down."
So, leaving the hot porridge to cool, the Three Bears set off for a walk in the woods.

They had not been gone two minutes, when the door of the cottage opened

and in came . . .

Goldilocks!

Goldilocks was a very naughty little girl.

First she jumped on Mr. Bear's big chair.

Next she jumped on Mrs. Bear's middle-size chair.

Then she jumped on Baby Bear's little chair and broke it!

Then Goldilocks spotted the Bears' breakfast on the table.

First she tried some of Mr. Bear's porridge.

Next she tried Mrs. Bear's porridge.

Then she tried Baby Bear's, and gobbled it all up!

All the porridge tasting had made Goldilocks feel very sleepy, so she went upstairs to have a nap.

First she got into Mr. Bear's big bed.

Next she got into Mrs. Bear's middle-size bed.

Finally she snuggled into Baby Bear's little bed.

"Perfect," said Goldilocks, and she instantly fell into a deep, deep sleep.

Meanwhile, farther up the road, Jack delivered a copy of the FAIRYTALE NEWS to Woodbine Cottage.

This was the cozy home of Mr. and Mrs. Hood and their daughter, Red Riding Hood.

While Mr. Hood read the latest sports news, Mrs. Hood handed a basket to Red Riding Hood. It was filled with a fruitcake, chocolate chip cookies, and a copy of KNITTER'S WEEKLY.

"Take this to your granny, dear," she said. "She's not very well and this will cheer her up."

"Okay, Mom," said Red Riding Hood, and off she went.

A short time later, deep in Tangled Wood, the Bears met Red Riding Hood, snacking from her basket.

"Hello, Bears," she said, still munching. "I'm off to see my granny – she isn't very well."

"Oh dear," said Mrs. Bear. "Give her our love."

And they waved goodbye.

However, no one noticed that hiding behind the bushes, Big Bad Wolf had heard every word.

A few minutes later, Big Bad Wolf met Jack on his paper rounds.

"Howdy, Jack," said Big Bad Wolf. "I'm off to visit Granny Hood—she's not feeling too good. Give me her newspaper and I'll take it for you."

"Okay, thanks," said Jack, and off he scooted. Moments later Big Bad Wolf knocked on the door of Granny's cottage.

"Who's there?" said Granny in a small, shaky voice. "It's the paperboy," Big Bad Wolf fibbed. "I've got your FAIRYTALE NEWS."

No sooner had Granny opened the door than Big Bad Wolf leaped inside and shoved poor Granny into a closet.

Then Big Bad Wolf put on Granny's spare bloomers and nightgown and hopped into her bed.

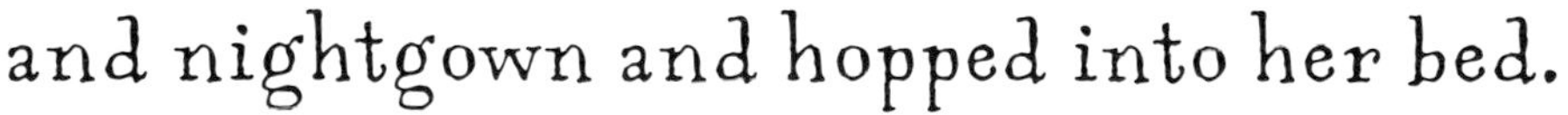

Big Bad Wolf made himself very comfy and settled down to read Granny's copy of the FAIRYTALE NEWS while he waited for little Red Riding Hood.

It wasn't very long before Red Riding Hood arrived at Granny's cottage and knocked on the door.

When she went inside, she saw a pair of big, hairy ears poking over the top of the newspaper.

"Oh! What big hairy ears you have, Granny," said Red Riding Hood.

"All the better to hear you with, my dear," growled Big Bad Wolf.

Red Riding Hood stared into Big Bad Wolf's huge eyes, gleaming behind Granny's spectacles.

"Oh! What big eyes you have, Granny," she said.

"All the better to see you with, my dear,"

growled Big Bad Wolf, licking his lips.

"And – oh! What big teeth you have, Granny!" said Red Riding Hood in a very wobbly voice.

"All the better to EAT you with!" roared Big Bad Wolf.

SUDDENLY the door crashed open!

There, filling the doorway, was Mr. Hood. He'd come over to bring Granny some wood for her fire.

"Hey! What's goin' on here?"

he roared as he swung his big ax.

Big Bad Wolf leaped straight out the window and ran off into the woods.

As he ran, he passed Jack, who was very surprised to see Big Bad Wolf in Granny's clothing.

Meanwhile . . .

after their long walk,
the Bears arrived back
at Honey Cottage to discover all was not as it should be.

"Someone's been eating my porridge!"
roared Mr. Bear.

"Someone's been eating MY porridge!"
growled Mrs. Bear.

"And someone's been eating my porridge and has eaten it all up!" sobbed Baby Bear.

"Someone's been sitting in my chair!"
roared Mr. Bear.

"Someone's been sitting in MY chair!"
growled Mrs. Bear.

"And someone's been sitting in my chair and broken it!" sobbed Baby Bear.

ZZZzzz

"And what's that noise?" said Mr. Bear.
"Sounds like someone snoring,"
said Mrs. Bear, and they all dashed
upstairs to the bedroom.

"Someone's been sleeping in my bed!" roared Mr. Bear.

"Someone's been sleeping in MY bed!" growled Mrs. Bear.

"And someone's been sleeping in my bed and is still in it!" yelled Baby Bear.

All this roaring and growling woke Goldilocks.

"Eeek!" she screamed,
and leaped out of bed and ran off!

Not far away, Jack was delivering his last copy of the FAIRYTALE NEWS—to his mom.

As Mrs. Hubbard read the market news in the paper, she said, "Look, Jack, cows are selling well. Why don't you take Daisy to town and try to get a good price for her?"

So Jack set off for the market with Daisy. Along the way they met a fast-talking stranger, who said, "I'll give you this magic bean for your fine cow, here and now. Whaddya say?"

"Okay, done!" said Jack. He took the magic bean, and the fast-talking stranger took Daisy.

When Jack got home, he gave his mom the magic bean. She was furious.

"You stupid boy," she roared. "You've been had!"

"But, but . . . it's a magic bean, Mom," stammered Jack.

"Magic bean? I'll give you magic bean!" said Jack's mom, throwing the bean out the window. "Look, it's disappeared!"

The next morning,

as Jack arrived back at Tumbledown Cottage after his paper rounds, he saw an enormous beanstalk growing in the garden.

"Wow!"

said Jack. "It WAS a magic bean." "Be careful," called his mom, as Jack began to climb the beanstalk. Higher and higher he went,

until . . .

eventually

he reached the top, where he found a huge castle. Inside the castle lived a giant— who, to Jack's horror, suddenly appeared, shouting,

"Fee, fi, fo, fum!"

Jack was so scared that he ran away to hide. But as he did so, he dropped his mom's newspaper.

"What's this?"

said the giant, as he bent down and picked up the newspaper. He'd never seen the FAIRYTALE NEWS before,

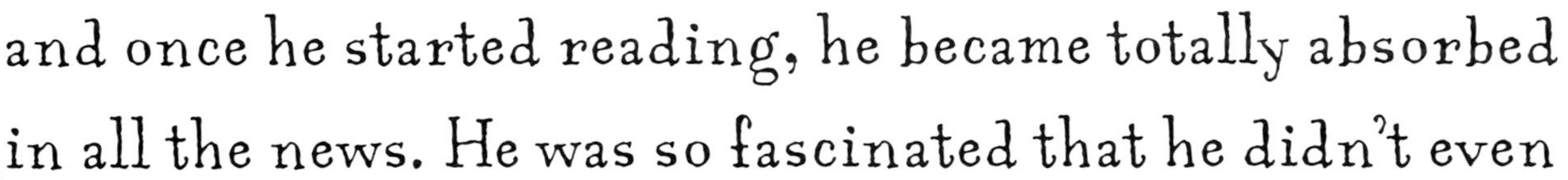

and once he started reading, he became totally absorbed in all the news. He was so fascinated that he didn't even notice Jack stealing away with his magic harp.

The next day . . .

Jack climbed
the beanstalk again,
carrying another copy
of the FAIRYTALE NEWS.

Again, the giant
appeared, shouting,

"Fee, fi, fo, fum!"

This time, however,
as Jack ran away, he dropped
the newspaper on purpose.
Again the giant picked it up, and
again he didn't notice when
Jack sneaked off with his hen
that laid golden eggs.

The following day, up Jack climbed again.

This time, however, when the giant appeared, shouting,

"Fee, fi, fo, fum!"

he didn't stop to read the FAIRYTALE NEWS

but chased Jack and caught him!

"Gotcha!" boomed the giant at a terrified Jack. "You're the one who's been stealin' my stuff. So I'm going to eat you up! Unless . . . you promise you'll climb up here every day with a copy of the FAIRYTALE NEWS. Whaddya say?"

Jack agreed and was as good as his word. Every morning he climbed the beanstalk with a newspaper for the giant, who always gave Jack a gold coin and a cup of juice.

Jack and his mom became very rich, but Jack still delivered the FAIRYTALE NEWS to Beanstalk Castle, as he so enjoyed going to see his best friend, the giant.

And, of course, they all lived happily ever after.

Established a long, long time ago

Charlie Wag ★ Fairyland's Top Newshound

Fair

The Top Stor

NABB
BIG BAD
ARRESTED IN

It looks as though B.B. W

Today, shortly after his relea
from jail on bail, B.B. Wolf
arrested yet again. B.B. Wolf
been in jail for blowing
the Little Pigs' houses. This tim
accused of impersonating Gran
locking her in a closet, wea
nightgown, and, worst of all,
to eat up Little Red Riding H
B.B. Wolf was found wear
nightgown, lacy nightcap, a

STOP PRESS

Blackbird Attack!

While the King was counting his money and the Queen was eating a honey sandwich, laundry maid Miss Rose Garden was washing the clothes, when, suddenly, down came a large blackbird that pecked her on the nose. The bird was thought to be one of twenty-four that had escaped from a six-penny pie made by Simple Simon.

Dr. Foster has put a vinegar-and-brown-paper bandage on Miss Garden's nose and advised her to stay indoors.

Udderly Ridiculous

It has been reported from Diddle Diddle Farm that a cow has jumped over the moon. At the scene we spoke to a little dog, who laughed and said,
nd a cat played the fiddle and
with the spoon! You

S

IN

and eat the farthing

PERTY FOR SALE

in need of
dy.

Today's

Today's rain will
but will come